SIXTY-MINU

THE TAMING OF THE SHREW

by Cass Foster

Sixty-Minute Shakespeare

The Taming of the Shrew

by Cass Foster

from The Taming of the Shrew
by William Shakespeare

Five Star Publications Inc.
A Resource for Every Author & Publisher Since 1985
Chandler, Arizona

Linda F. Radke, President
Five Star Publications, Inc.
P.O. Box 6698
Chandler, AZ 85246-6698
(480) 940-8182
www.FiveStarPublications.com

www.GetShakespeare.com

Library of Congress Cataloging-in-Publication Data

Publisher's Cataloging-In-Publication Data

Shakespeare, William, 1564-1616.
The taming of the shrew / [abridged] by Cass Foster ; from The taming of the shrew by William Shakespeare.

p. ; cm. -- (Sixty-minute Shakespeare)

Issued also as an ebook.
Summary: An abridged version of Shakespeare's comedy about love, marriage, money, disguises, and the wooing and taming of strong-willed Kate.
Interest grade level: 6 & up.
ISBN-13: 978-1-58985-220-4
ISBN-10: 1-58985-220-6
eISBN: 978-1-58985-221-1

1. Man-woman relationships--Juvenile drama. 2. Married people--Italy--Padua--Juvenile drama. 3. Padua (Italy)--Juvenile drama. 4. Sex role--Juvenile drama. 5. Man-woman relationships--Drama. 6. Marriage--Italy--Padua--Drama. 7. Sex role--Drama. I. Foster, Cass, 1948- II. Title.

PR2832 .A25 2012
822.3/3 2012938451

Electronic edition provided by:

eStarPublish.com

The eBook Division of Five Star Publications, Inc.

Printed in the United States of America

Cover Design: Kris Taft Miller
Page Layout: Linda Longmire
Editor: Cristy Bertini
Proofreader: Patricia Kot
Project Manager: Patti Crane

Dedicated with Love to My
Five Amazing Grandchildren

Jason, Tesla, Mykena, Trevyn & Tucker

WELCOME TO THE SIXTY-MINUTE SHAKESPEARE

Thanks to the progressive thinking of so many curriculum developers, Language Arts people and the splendid film work being done by directors such as Kenneth Branagh and Franco Zeffirelli, there has been a phenomenal growth in interest in Shakespeare.

No playwright, past or present, approaches the brilliance and magnitude of William Shakespeare. What other individual has even come close to understanding and then dramatizing the human condition? Just for the fun of it, I am listing (following these introductory remarks) a sample of themes and images so richly developed in the canon of his plays.

Shakespeare's characters are so well-rounded and beautifully constructed that it is common to see them as actual historical figures. When someone mentions Hamlet, Iago, Ophelia, or Puck, we immediately experience images and emotions that come from memories of people we know. We may feel compassion, frustration, sorrow, or pleasure.

As one of the wealthiest people of his time, Shakespeare earned his living as a playwright, theatre manager, actor, and shareholder in the Globe Theatre. He worked tirelessly to entertain. (Theatres presented a new play every day and the average new play had a total of only ten performances over an entire season.) He rebelled against the contemporary theatrical standards (the neo-classical principles that limited dramatic structure throughout France and Italy), he took plots from other published works (making them uniquely his own), and he created a spectacle (without the use of elaborate scenery) to captivate audiences of all social levels.

Imagine the challenge in quieting a crowd of three thousand in a theatre where vendors sell wine, beer, ale, nuts, and cards; where there is no intermission; where birds fly overhead; and where audience members stand near performers. Such was the setting in which Shakespeare's plays were originally staged.

The world's most familiar and successful wordsmith used language to skillfully create images, plot, and a sense of music and rhythm. The purpose behind this series is to reduce (not contemporize) the language. The unabridged Shakespeare simply isn't practical in all situations. Not all educators or directors have the luxury of time to explore the entire text. This is not intended to be a substitute for a thorough study of Shakespeare. It is merely a stepping stone.

I challenge each of you to go beyond the Sixty-Minute versions. Use the comfort, appreciation, and self-confidence you will gain to go further. Be proud of the insights and knowledge you acquire, but do not be satisfied. The more you read, the more you gain.

May each of you be blessed with an abundance of good health and happiness. I thank you for your interest in our work and hope you are pleased with what we have done.

May the Verse Be With You!

A COUPLE OF STAGING CONSIDERATIONS

Scenery

There are two excellent reasons theatres rarely use much scenery when staging Shakespeare. The first is related to the number of changes required. If we have to wait every five to ten minutes to watch scenery struck and set up, we end up watching a play about moving lumber. The second is because the audience will lose sight of what the play is about. Audiences need a couple minutes to adjust to the new scenic look of a dazzling waterfall and lush forest. By the time they take it all in and start paying attention to what the actors are saying, it is time to set up the next scene and the audience will be lost.

Location is normally established through dialogue and the use of a few simple props: a throne-like chair for the king's court, a long table with benches for an inn, or a bed for the queen's bed chamber. The key is to keep it simple.

Pacing

You will want to keep things moving all the time. That doesn't mean actors should talk and move quickly; it simply means one scene should flow smoothly to the next without delay or interruption.

As Scene One ends, the actors pick up their props and walk off. Actors for Scene Two enter from a different direction with their props and begin dialogue as soon as they enter the acting area, putting their props in place as they speak. Yes, the audience will still have view of the actors from the first scene, but they will gladly accept this convention if it means taking fifteen minutes off performance time.

IMAGES AND THEMES TO LOOK FOR IN THE VARIOUS PLAYS

Mistaken identity	Irresponsible power
Wisdom of fools	Destiny or fate
Insanity	Real or pretended madness
Greed and corruption	Ambition
Religious persecution	Tyranny
The elements	Types of love
The supernatural	Abusive Relationships
Darkness and light	Foils or opposites
Loneliness or isolation	Spying
Anti-Semitism	Paranoia
Conspiracy	Play-acting
Revenge	Justice
Hypocrisy	Heavenly retribution
Abandonment	Forgiveness
Pride	Witchcraft
Honor	Mortality
Violence	Self-destruction
Bravery	Black or white magic
Rebellion	Animals
Savagery	Nature
Seduction	Reality vs. illusion
Disease or physical decay	Astrological influence
Loyalty	Characters reforming
War	Old age
Marriage	Freedom
False accusations	Usurping of power

Fertility suppression
Sexual misadventure
Melancholy
Corrupt society
Love and/or friendship
Multiple meanings of words
Thought vs. action
Impetuous love
Role of women
Human frailty
Preparing for leadership
Charity/Betrayal
Impact of money
Social status
Changing identities
Deception
Madness
Narrow mindedness
Self-righteousness
Suicide
Maturity
Love of money
Supernatural
Power of evil
Temptation
Courage
Character
Regicide
Loss of one's soul
Prophecies

THE COMPLETE WORKS OF WILLIAM SHAKESPEARE

1589 - 1591	Henry VI, Part 1, 2 and 3
1592 - 1593	Richard III
1593 - 1594	Titus Andronicus
1592 - 1594	Comedy of Errors
1593 - 1594	Taming of the Shrew
1594	The Two Gentlemen of Verona
1594 - 1595	Love's Labour's Lost
1594 - 1596	King John
1595	Richard II
1595 - 1596	A Midsummer Night's Dream
1595 - 1596	Romeo and Juliet
1596 - 1597	The Merchant of Venice
1597	The Merry Wives of Windsor
1597 - 1598	Henry IV, Part 1 and 2
1598 - 1599	Much Ado About Nothing
1599	Henry V
1599	Julius Caesar
1599	As You Like It
1600 - 1601	Hamlet
1601 - 1602	Twelfth Night
1601 - 1602	Troilus and Cressida
1602 - 1603	All's Well That Ends Well
1604	Measure for Measure
1604	Othello
1605	The Tragedy of King Lear
1606	Macbeth
1606 - 1607	Antony and Cleopatra

1607 - 1608	Timon of Athens
1607 - 1608	Pericles, Prince of Tyre
1607 - 1608	Coriolanus
1609 - 1610	Cymbeline
1609 - 1610	The Winter's Tale
1611	The Tempest
1612 - 1613	Henry VIII
1613	Two Noble Kinsmen (Authorship in question)

23 April 1564 - 23 April 1616

"If we wish to know the force of human genius, we should read Shakespeare. If we wish to see the insignificance of human learning, we may study his commentators."

William Hazlitt (1778-1830) English Essayist. "On the Ignorance of the Learned," in Edinburgh Magazine (July 1818).

COMMON QUOTES FROM THE BARD

Romeo and Juliet

Parting is such sweet sorrow.
A plague o' both your houses.
O Romeo, Romeo! Wherefore art thou Romeo?

A Midsummer Night's Dream

Lord, what fools these mortals be.
The course of true love never did run smooth.
To say the truth, reason and love keep little company
together now-a-days.

As You Like It

All that glisters is not gold.
Love is blind.
All the world's a stage
And all the men and women merely players.
For ever and a day.

Twelfth Night

Some are born great, some achieve greatness, and some
have greatness thrust upon them.
Out of the jaws of death.
O, had I but followed the arts!
Many a good hanging prevents a bad marriage.

Henry IV; Part 1

The better part of valor is discretion.
To give the devil his due.
He hath eaten me out of house and home.

Henry VI, Part 2

Let's kill all the lawyers.

The Merry Wives of Windsor

Better three hours too soon than a minute too late.

Casablanca

This could be the start of a beautiful friendship.

Macbeth

Out, damned spot! Out, I say!
Screw your courage to the sticking place.

Hamlet

Something is rotten in the state of Denmark.
To be or not to be. That is the question.
The lady doth protest too much, methinks.
Good night, sweet prince, And flights of
angels sing thee to thy rest!

The Merchant of Venice

The devil can cite scriptures for his purpose.

Pericles

Few love to hear the sins they love to act.

Richard III

Now is the winter of our discontent.
Off with his head!
A horse! A horse! My kingdom for a horse.

Julius Caesar

Beware the ides of March.
Friends, Romans, countrymen, lend me your ears.
It was Greek to me.

Much Ado About Nothing

The world must be peopled. When I said I would die a bachelor, I did not think I should live till I were married.

Measure for Measure

The miserable have no other medicine but only hope.

Troilus and Cressida

To fear the worst oft cures the worse.

The Comedy of Errors

Unquiet meals make ill digestions.

CAST OF CHARACTERS

Messenger
CHRISTOPHER SLY, a tinker
BAPTISTA, a wealthy gentleman of Padua
VINCENTIO, an old gentleman of Pisa
LUCENTIO, son of Vincentio, in love with Bianca
PETRUCHIO, a gentleman of Verona, suitor of Katherina
GREMIO, suitor to Bianca
HORTENSIO, suitor to Bianca
TRANIO, servant to Lucentio
BIONDELLO, servant to Lucentio
GRUMIO, servant to Petruchio
CURTIS, servant to Petruchio
A Pedant
KATHERINA, the Shrew daughter of Baptista
BIANCA, daughter of Baptista
Widow (Only if staging Act V, Scene 2)
Tailor, Haberdasher and Servants attending Baptista and Petruchio

Double-casting suggestions:
Genders can be whatever directors choose. Just please don't "pretend" to be another gender or act silly.

Male - Baptista/Lucentio Petruchio/Sly Gremio Hortensio Vincentio

Female - Haberdasher/Widow Katherina Bianca

M or F - Biondello/Curtis Servants (4-6) Tranio Pedant/Tailor Grumio/Induction Servant

SCENE

PADUA AND PETRUCHIO'S COUNTRY HOUSE

INDUCTION

BEFORE AN ALEHOUSE ON A HEATH

Enter Christopher Sly

Sly. I am Christopher Sly. Call me not "Honor" nor "Lordship". I ne'er drank sack in my life. And if you give me any conserves, give me conserves of beef*. Ne'er ask me what raiment I'll wear, for I have no more doublets than backs, no more stockings than legs, nor no more shoes than feet, nay sometime more feet than shoes, or such shoes as my toes look through the overleather.
What would you make me mad? Am not I Christopher Sly, old Sly's son, of Burton Heath, by birth a peddler, by education a cardmaker*, by transmutation a bearheard*, and now by present profession a tinker? Ask Marian Hacket, the fat alewife of Wincot, if she know me not. What! I am not bestraught*. Nay...

Enter Messenger

Messenger. Your Honor's players are come to play a pleasant comedy,
For so your doctors hold it very meet,
Seeing too much sadness hath congealed your blood,
And melancholy is the nurse of frenzy.
Therefore, they thought it good you hear a play
And frame your mind to mirth and merriment,
Which bars a thousand harms and lengthens life.

conserves of beef: salted beef **cardmaker:** maker of cards for combing wool. **bearheard:** bear-handler **bestraught:** distracted.

Sly. Merry, I will. Let them play it for we shall ne'er be younger. Let the merriment begin: A play within a play.

They both exit.

ACT 1, SCENE 1

A PUBLIC PLACE

Enter LUCENTIO and his man TRANIO.

Lucentio. Tranio, since for the great desire I had
To see fair Padua, nursery of arts,
I am arrived for fruitful Lombardy,
The pleasant garden of great Italy,
And by my father's love and leave am armed
With his good will and thy good company,
My trusty servant, well approved* in all,
Here let us breathe* and haply* institute
A course of learning and ingenious* studies.
And therefore, Tranio, for the time I study,
Virtue and that part of philosophy
Will I apply* that treats of happiness
By virtue specially to be achieved.

Tranio. Mi perdonato*, gentle master mine;
I am in all affected as yourself,
Glad that you thus continue your resolve
To suck the sweets of sweet philosophy.

Lucentio. But stay awhile. What company is this?

They move to the side as Baptista, Katherina, Bianca, Gremio and Hortensio enter.

approved: confirmed **breathe:** pause **haply:** perhaps
ingenious: intellectual **apply:** address myself to **Mi perdonato:** pardon me

Baptista. Gentlemen, importune* me no further,
For how I firmly am resolved you know,
Before I have a husband for the elder.
If either of you both love Katherina,
Because I know you well and love you well,
Leave shall you have to court her at your pleasure.
Gremio. To cart her* rather; she's too rough for me.
There, there, Hortensio, will you any wife?

Katherina. I pray you, sir, is it your will
To make a stale* of me amongst these mates?

Hortensio. Mates, maid! How mean you that? No mates for you,
Unless you were of gentler, milder mold.

Katherina. I' faith, sir, you shall never need to fear.
I wis* it is not halfway to her heart.
But if it were, doubt not her care should be
To comb your noddle* with a three-legged stool
And paint your face* and use you like a fool.

Hortensio. From all such devils. Good Lord deliver us!

Gremio. And me too, good Lord!

Tranio. Master! Here's some good pastime toward.
That wrench is stark mad or wonderful froward*.

importune: ask someone persistently **cart her:** transport in an open cart subjecting women of ill-repute to shame **stale:** butt or prostitute **I wis:** certainly **noddle:** a person's head **paint your face:** i.e., with bleeding scratches **froward:** perverse

Lucentio. But in the other's silence do I see
Maid's mild behavior and sobriety.

Baptista. Gentlemen, that I may soon make good,
What I have said - Bianca get you in,
And let it not displease thee, good Bianca,
For I will love thee ne'er the less, my girl.
My books and instruments shall be my company,
On them to look and practice by myself.

Katherina. A pretty pet! It is best
Put finger in the eye, and she knew why.

Bianca. Sister, content you in my discontent.
Sir, to your pleasure I humbly subscribe.

Lucentio. Hark, Tranio! Thou mayst hear Minerva* speak.

Hortensio. Signior Baptista, will you be so strange?
Sorry am I that our good will effects
Bianca's grief.

Gremio. Why will you mew her up*,
Signior Baptista, for this fiend of hell,
And make her bear the penance of her tongue?

Minerva: patroness of arts and goddess of wisdom **mew her up:** confine her

Baptista. Gentlemen. Content ye; I am resolved.
Go in Bianca. *She exits.*
And for I know she taketh most delight
In music, instruments and poetry,
Schoolmasters will I keep within my house
Fit to instruct her youth. If you, Hortensio,
Or, Signior Gremio, you, know any such,
Prefer* them hither; for to cunning* men
I will be very kind and liberal
To mine own children in good bringing up.
And so, farewell. Katherina, you may stay,
For I have more to commune with Bianca.
He exits.

Katherina. Why, and I trust I may go too, may I not?
What! Shall I be appointed hours as though, belike*,
I knew not what to take and what to leave? Ha!
She exits.

Hortensio. Signior Gremio; but a word, I pray.
Though the nature of our quarrel yet never brooked* parle*, know now, upon advice, it toucheth us both that we may yet again have access to our fair mistress and be happy rivals in Bianca's love - to labor and effect one thing specially.

Gremio. What' that, I pray?

Hortensio. Marry, sir, to get a husband for her sister.

Gremio. A husband? A devil.

Hortensio. I say, a husband.

Prefer: recommend **cunning:** clever **belike:** probably, perhaps
brooked: endured **parle:** consultation

Gremio. I say, a devil. Thinkst thou, Hortensio, though her father be very rich, any man is so very a fool to be married to hell?

Hortensio. Tush, Gremio! Though it past your patience and mine to endure her loud alarums*, why, man, there be good fellow in the world, an a man could light on them, would take her with all her faults, and money enough.

Gremio. I cannot tell; but I had as lief* take her dowry* with this condition: to be whipped at the high cross every morning.

Hortensio. Faith, as you say, there's small choice in rotten apples. But come, since this bar in law makes us friends, it shall be so far forth friendly maintained, till by helping Baptista's eldest daughter to a husband we set his youngest free for a husband, and then have to 't fresh. Sweet Bianca! Happy man be his dole! He that runs fastest gets the ring. How say you, Signior Gremio?

Gremio. I am agreed. And would I have given him the best horse in Padua to begin his wooing that would thoroughly woo her, wed her, and bed her, and rid the house of her. Come on.

They exit.

Tranio. Pray sir, tell me, is it possible
That love should of a sudden take such hold?

alarums: disturbances **lief:** gladly; willingly **dowry:** money, goods, or estate that a woman brings to her husband in marriage

Lucentio. O Tranio! Till I found it to be true
I never thought it possible or likely.
Tranio, I burn, I pine, I perish, Tranio,
If I achieve not tis young modest girl.

Tranio. Master, you looked so longly* on the maid,
Perhaps you marked not what's the pith* of all.

Lucentio. O, yes, I saw sweet beauty in her face.

Tranio. Saw you no more? Marked you not how her
sister Began to scold and raise up such a storm. That
mortal ears might hardly endure the din?

Lucentio. Tranio, I saw her coral lips to move
And with her breath she did perfume the air.
Sacred and sweet was all I saw in her.

Tranio. *(Aside)* Then tis time to stir him from his trance.
(To Luc) I pray, awake sir! If you love the maid,
Bend thoughts and wits to achieve her. Thus it stands:
Her elder sister is so curst* and shrewd*
That till the father rid his hands of her,
Master, your love must live a maid at home;
But therefore has he closely mewed her up,
Because* she will not be annoyed by suitors.

Lucentio. Ah, Tranio, what a cruel father's he!
But art thou not advised he took some care
To get her cunning schoolmasters to instruct her?

Tranio. Ay, marry, am I, sir, and now 'tis plotted.

Lucentio. I have it, Tranio.

longly: lingeringly **pith:** essence **curst:** ill-tempered **shrewd:** disagreeable
because: so that

Tranio. Master, for my hand*,
Both our inventions meet and jump in.

Lucentio. Tell me thine first.

Tranio. You will be schoolmaster
And undertake the teaching of the maid;
That's your device.

Lucentio. It is. May it be done?

Tranio. Not possible. For who shall bear your part
And be in Padua here Vencentio's son;
Keep house and ply his book, welcome his friends,
Visit his countrymen and banquet them.

Lucentio. Basta*, content thee; for I have it full*.
We have not yet been seen in any house,
Nor can we be distinguished by our faces
For man or master. Then, it follows thus:
Thou shalt be master, Tranio, in my stead.
'Tis hatched and shall be so. Tranio, at once
Uncase thee. Take my colored hat and cloak.
When Biondello comes he waits on thee,
But I will charm him first to keep his tongue.

Tranio. For so your father charged me at our parting:
"Be serviceable to my son," quoth he,
Although I think 'twas in another sense -
I am content to be Lucentio,
Because I so well love Lucentio.

Lucentio. And let me be a slave, t'achieve that maid
Whose sudden sight hath thralled my wounded eye.
Here comes the rogue.

for my hand: I'll bet anything **basta:** enough **I have it full:** see the whole plan

Enter Biondello

Lucentio. Sirrah, where have you been?

Biondello. Where have I been! Nay, how now! Where
are you?
Master, has my fellow Tranio stol'n your clothes,
Or you stol'n his? Or both? Pray, what's the news?

Lucentio. Sirrah, come hither: tis no time to jest,
Your fellow Tranio here, to save my life,
Puts my apparel and my count'nance* on,
And I, for my escape, put on his.

Lucentio. For in a quarrel since I came ashore
I killed a man and fear I was descried.
Wait you on him, I charge you, as becomes,
While I make way from hence to save my life,
You understand me?

Biondello. I, sir! ne'er a whit.

Lucentio. And not a jot of "Tranio" in your mouth.
Tranio is changed into Lucentio.

Tranio. When I am alone, why, then I am Tranio;
But in all places else, your master Lucentio.

Lucentio. Let's go.

All three exit.

count'nance: semblance

ACT I, SCENE 2

PADUA. BEFORE HORTENSIO'S HOUSE

Enter Petruchio and his man, Grumio

Petruchio. Verona, for a while I take my leave
To see my friends in Padua; but of all,
My best beloved and approved friend,
Hortensio; and I trow* this in his house.
Here, sirrah Grumio; knock I say.

Grumio. Knock, sir? Whom should I knock?

Petruchio. Villain, I say. Knock me here soundly.

Grumio. Knock you here, sir?

Petruchio. Villain, I say, knock me at this gate,
And rap me well or I'll knock your knave's pate*.

Grumio. My master has grown quarrelsome. I should knock you first.

*Petruchio wrings him by the ears***.

Grumio. Help, masters. Help! My master is mad.

He shoves Grumio to the ground and Hortensio enters.
Hortensio. How now, what's the matter? My old friend Grumio! And my good friend Petruchio. How do you all at Verona?

Petruchio. Signior Hortensio, come you to part the fray?

trow: think **pate:** head
** *See section back of script on Stage Combat.*

Hortensio. Rise, Grumio, rise; we will compound* this quarrel.

Petruchio. I bade the rascal knock upon your gate,
And could not get him for my heart to do it.

Grumio. Knock at the gate? O' heavens! Spake you not these words plain.

Petruchio. Sirrah, be gone, or talk not, I advise you.

Hortensio. Petruchio, patience. I am Grumio's pledge.
And tell me now, sweet friend, what happy gale
Blows you to Padua here from Verona?

Petruchio. Antonio, my father, is deceased
And I have thrust myself unto this maze,
Happily to wive and thrive as best I may.

Hortensio. Petruchio, shall I then come roundly to thee
And wish thee to a shrewd ill-favored wife?
Thou'dst thank me but a little for my counsel,
And yet I'll promise thee she shall be rich,
And very rich; but thou'rt too much my friend,
And I'll not wish thee to her.

Petruchio. Signior Hortensio, 'twixt such friends as we,
Few words suffice; and therefore, if thou know
One rich enough to be Petruchio's wife,
I come to wive it wealthily in Padua.

compound: settle

Hortensio. I can, Petruchio, help thee to a wife
With wealth enough, and young and beauteous,
Brought up as best becomes a gentlewoman.
Her only fault - and that is faults enough -
Is that she is intolerable curst
And shrewd and froward*, so beyond all measure
That, were my state far worser that it is,
I would not wed her for a mine of gold.

Petruchio. Hortensio, peace! Thou knowst not gold's
effect.Tell me her father's name, and 'tis enough;
For I will board her though she chide as loud
As thunder when the clouds in autumn crack.

Hortensio. Her father is Baptista Minola,
An affable and courteous gentleman;
Her name is Katherina Minola,
Renowned in Padua for her scolding tongue.

Petruchio. I know her father, though I know not her.
I will not sleep, Hortensio, till I see her.

Hortensio. Tarry*, Petruchio. I will go with thee,
For in Baptista's keep my treasure is.
He hath the jewel of my life in hold,
His youngest daughter, beautiful Bianca,
And therefore this order hath Baptista ta'en,
That none shall have access unto Bianca
Till Katharine the curst have got a husband.

Grumio. Katherine the curst!
A title for a maid of all titles the worst.

froward: obstinate **tarry:** stay longer than intended

Hortensio. Now shall my friend Petruchio do me grace,
And offer me disguised in sober robes,
To old Baptista as a schoolmaster
Well seen in music, to instruct Bianca,
That so I may, by this device, at least
Have leave and leisure to make love to her,
And, unsuspected, court her by herself.

Grumio. Here's no knavery! See, to beguile the old folks, how the
young folks lay their heads together! Master, master,
look about you. Who goes there, ha?

Enter Gremio and Lucentio (disguised as Cambio)

Hortensio. Peace, Grumio! It is the rival of my love.

Petruchio. Peace, sirrah!

Hortensio. Grumio, mum! G-d* save you, Signior Gremio!

Gremio. And you are well met, Signior Hortensio!
Trow you wither I am going? To Baptista Minola.
I promised to inquire carefully
About a schoolmaster for the fair Bianca,
And, by good fortune, I have lighted well
On this young man; for learning and behavior
Fit for her turn; well read in poetry
And other books, good ones, I warrant ye.

G-d: Cass's religious beliefs include once the name G-d is spelled out fully the text cannot be discarded, dropped or disrespected.

Hortensio. 'Tis well; and I have met a gentleman
Hath promised me to help me to another,
A fine musician to instruct our mistress;
So shall I no whit be behind in duty
To fair Bianca, so beloved of me.

Gremio. Beloved of me, and that my deeds shall prove.

Hortensio. Listen to me, and if you speak me fair
I'll tell you news indifferent good for either.
Here is a gentleman whom by chance I met,
Upon agreement from us to his liking,
Will undertake to woo curst Katherine;
Yea, and to marry her if her dowry please.

Gremio. So said, so done, is well.
Hortensio, have you told him all her faults?

Petruchio. I know she is an irksome, brawling scold:
If that be all, masters, I hear no harm.

Gremio. O, sir, such a life, with such a wife, were strange!
Will you woo this wildcat?

Petruchio. Will I live?
Why came I hither but to that intent?
Think you a little din can daunt my ears?
Have I not in my time heard lions roar?
Have I not heard great ordnance* in the field
And heaven's artillery thunder in the skies?
Tush, tush! Fear boys with bugs.

Grumio. *(Aside)* For he fears none.

Enter Tranio (as Lucentio) and Biondello.

ordnance: cannons

Tranio. Gentlemen, G-d save you! If I may be bold,
Tell me, I beseech you, which is the readiest way
To the house of Baptista Minola? He that has the two fair daughters.

Hortensio. Are you a suitor to the maid you talk of, yea or no?

Tranio. And if I be, sire, is it any offense?

Gremio. No, if without more words you will get you hence.

Tranio. Why, sir, I pray, are not the streets as free
For me as for you?

Gremio. But so is not she.
That she's the choice love of Signior Gremio.

Hortensio. That she's the chosen of Signior Hortensio.

Tranio. Softly, my masters. If you be gentlemen,
Do me this right: hear me with patience.
Baptista is a noble gentleman,
And were his daughters fairer than she is
She may more suitors have, and me for one.

Hortensio. Sir, let me be so bold as ask you,
Did you yet ever see Baptista's daughter?

Tranio. No, sir, but hear I do that he hath two,
The one as famous for a scolding tongue
As is the other for beauteous modesty.

Petruchio. Sir, sir, the first's for me; let her go by.
The youngest daughter, whom you harken for,
Her father keeps from all access of suitors,
And will not promise her to any man
Upon the elder sister first be wed;
The younger then is free, and not before.

Tranio. If it be so, sir, that you are the man
Must stead us all, and me amongst the rest;
And if you break the ice and do this feat,
Achieve the elder, set the younger free
For our access, whose hap shall be to have her
Will not so graceless be to be ingrate.

Hortensio. You must, as we do, gratify this gentleman,
To whom we all rest generally beholding.

Tranio. Sir, I shall not be slack; in sign whereof,
Please ye we may contrive* this afternoon
And quaff carouses* to our mistress' health,
And do as adversaries do in law*,
Strive mightily, but eat and drink as friends.

Grumio. O excellent motion! Fellows, let's be gone.

Hortensio. The motion's good indeed, and be it so -
Petruchio, I shall be your ben venuto*.

They all exit.

contrive: pass the time **quaff carouses:** drink heartedly
adversaries do in law: i.e. lawyers on opposite sides of a case
ben venuto: welcomer, i.e. to properly introduce him

ACT II, SCENE 1

Padua. A Room in BAPTISTA'S House

Enter Katherina dragging in Bianca.

Bianca. Good sister, wrong me not, nor wrong yourself
Or what you will command me will I do,
So well I know my duty to my elders.

Katherina. Of all thy suitors, here I charge thee, tell
Whom thou lovest best; see thou dissemble not.

Bianca. Believe me sister, of all the men alive
I never yet beheld that special face
Which I could fancy more than any other.

Katherina. Thou liest.

Katherina pushes Bianca as Baptista enters.

Baptista. Why, how now, dame! When grows this insolence? Why dost thou wrong her that did ne'er wrong thee?

Katherina. Her silence flouts me, and I'll be revenged.

Katherina chases Bianca and finally Baptista holds her back.

Baptista. What! In my sight? Bianca, get thee in.

Bianca exits.

Katherina. What! You will not suffer me? Nay, now I see
She is your treasure, she must have a husband;
I must dance barefoot on her wedding day.
Talk not to me. I will go sit and weep.

Katherina exits as enters Gremio, Lucenti (Gambio); Petruchio and Hortensio (Licio) as a musician and Tranio (Lucentio) with his boy, Biondello, bearing a lute and books.

Gremio. Good morrow, neighbor Baptista.

Baptista. Good morrow, neighbor Gremio. G-d save you, gentlemen!

Petruchio. And you, good sir. Pray, have you not a daughter Called Katherina, fair and virtuous?

Baptista. I have a daughter, sir, called Katherina.

Petruchio. I am a gentleman of Verona, sir.
That, hearing of her beauty and her wit,
Her affability and bashful modesty,
Her wondrous qualities and mild behavior,
Am bold to show myself a forward guest
Within your house, to make mine eye the witness
Of that report which I so oft have heard.
And, for an entrance to my entertainment*,
I do present you with a man of mine.

Presenting Hortensio.

Cunning in music and the mathematics,
To instruct her fully in those sciences,
Accept of him, or else you do me wrong,
His name is Licio, born in Mantua.

Baptista. Y'are welcome, sir, and he for your good sake.
But for my daughter Katherina, this I know,
She is not for your turn, the more my grief.

entrance to my entertainment: entrance fee

Petruchio. I see you do not mean to part with her,
Or else you like not my company.

Baptista. Mistake me not. I speak but as I find.
Whence are you, sir. What may I call your name?

Petruchio. Petruchio is my name, Antonio's son,
A man well known throughout all Italy.

Baptista. I know him well. You are welcome for his sake.

Gremio. Let us, that are poor petitioners, speak too. Neighbor, this is a gift very grateful, I am sure of it. To express the like kindness, myself, that have been more kindly beholding to you than any, freely give unto you this young scholar.

Presenting "Lucentio"

That hath been long studying at Rheims; as cunning in Greek, Latin, and other languages, as the other in music and mathematics. His name is Cambio; pray accept his service.

Baptista. A thousand thanks, Signior Gremio. Welcome, good Cambio. (To Tranio) But may I be so bold as to know the cause of your coming?

Tranio/Luc. Pardon me, sir. The boldness is mine own,
That, being a stranger in this city here,
Do make myself a suitor to your daughter,
Unto Bianca, fair and virtuous.
Nor is your firm resolve unknown to me
In the preferment of the eldest sister.
This liberty is all that I request,
That, upon knowledge of my parentage,
I may have welcome 'mongst the rest that woo,
And free access and favor as the rest.
And, toward the education of your daughters,
I here bestow a simple instrument,
And this small packet of Greek and Latin books;
If you accept them, then their worth is great.

Baptista. Lucentio is your name, of whence, I pray?

Tranio/Luc. Of Pisa, sir, son to Vincentio.

Baptista. A mighty man of Pisa; by report
I know him well. You are very welcome, sir.
(To Hortensio) Take you that lute, (To Luc) and you
the rest of the books. You shall go see your pupils
presently. Holla, within!

Enter a servant.

Baptista. Sirrah, lead these gentlemen
To my daughters, and tell them both
These are their tutors: bid them use them well.

Exit servant followed by Lucentio, Hortensio and Biondello.

Baptista. We will go walk in the orchard
And then to dinner.

Petruchio. Signior Baptista, my business asketh haste
And every day I cannot come to woo.
Then tell me, if I get your daughter's love,
What dowry shall I have with her to wife?

Baptista. After my death the one half of my lands,
And, in possession, twenty thousand crowns.

Petruchio. And, for that dowry, I'll assure her of
Her widowhood, be it that she survive me,
In all my lands and leases whatsoever.
Let specialties* be therefore drawn between us
That covenants may be kept on either hand.

Baptista. Ay, when the special thing is well obtained,
That is, her love; for that is all in all.

Petruchio. I am as peremptory* as she proud-minded;
And where two raging fires meet together
They do consume the thing that feeds their fury:
For I am rough and woo not like a babe.

Baptista. Well mayst thou woo and happy be thy speed!
But be thou armed for some unhappy words.

Enter Hortensio (Lucio) with his head bandaged

Baptista. How now, my friend! Why dost thou look so pale?

Hortensio/Luc. For fear, I promise you.

Baptista. What, will my daughter prove a good musician?

specialties: contracts **peremptory:** insisting on immediate attention or obedience

Hortensio/Luc. I think she'll sooner prove a soldier.

Baptista. Why, then thou canst not break her to the lute?

Hortensio/Luc. Why no; for she hath broke the lute to me.

Petruchio. Now, by the world, it is a lusty wench!
I love her ten times more than e'er I did:
O, how I long to have some chat with her!

Baptista. Well, go with me, and be not so discomfited.
Proceed in practice with my younger daughter;
She apt to learn and thankful for good turns.
Signior Petruchio, will you go with us,
Or shall I send my daughter Kate to you?

Petruchio. I pray you do I will attend her here.

Exit all but Petruchio.

Say that she rail, why then I'll tell her plain
She sings as sweetly as a nightingale.
Say that she frown; I'll say she looks as clear*
As morning roses newly washed with dew.
Say she be mute and will not speak a word;
Then I'll commend her volubility*.
If she bid me pack, I'll bid her thanks,
As though she bid me stay by her a week.
But here she comes;

Katherina enters.

clear: cheerful **volubility:** rapid and fluent speaking

Petruchio. Good morrow, Kate; for that's your name, I hear.

Katherina. Well have you heard, but something hard of hearing. They call me Katherina that do talk to me.

Petruchio. You lie, in faith, for you are called plain Kate,
And bonny Kate, and sometimes Kate the curst;
But, Kate, the prettiest Kate in Christendom;
Kate of Kate Hall, my super-dainty Kate,
For dainties are all Kates - and therefore, Kate,
Take this of me, Kate of my consolation:
Hearing the mildness praised in every town,
Thy virtues spoke of and they beauty sounded -
Myself am moved to woo thee for my wife.

Katherina. Moved! In good time: let him that moved you hither. Remove you hence. I knew you at the first You were a movable.

Petruchio. Why, what's a movable?

Katherina. A joint stool.

Petruchio. Thou hast hit it, come sit on me.

Brings her down to his lap.

Katherina. Asses are made to bear, and so are you.

Petruchio. Women are made to bear* and so are you.

Katherina. No jade* as you, if me you mean.

Petruchio. Alas, good Kate. I will not burden thee;
For, knowing thee to be but young and light...

bear: bear children **jade:** a horse that soon tires

She pushes him down and rises.

Katherina. Too light for such a swain* as you to catch,
And yet as heavy as my weight should be.

Petruchio. Come, come you wasp. I'faith you are too angry.

Katherina. If I be waspish, best beware my sting.

Petruchio. My remedy is then to pluck it out.

Katherina. Ay, if the fool could find it where it lies.

Petruchio. Who knows not where a wasp does wear his sting?
In his tail.

Katherina. In his tongue.

Petruchio. Whose tongue?

Katherina. Yours if you talk of tales; and so, farewell.

Petruchio. What! With my tongue in your tail? Nay, come again.
Good Kate. I am a gentleman.

Kate. That I'll try.

*Kate slaps him***.

Petruchio. I swear I'll cuff you, if you strike again.

Katherina. If you strike me, you are no gentleman.

swain: a male lover or admirer ** See section back of script on Stage Combat

Petruchio. Nay, come, Kate, come. You must not look so sour.

Katherina. It is my fashion when I see a crab.

Kate attempts to slap Petruchio, but he catches her arm.

Petruchio. Why, there's no crab, and therefore look not sour.

Katherina. There is, there is.

Petruchio. Then show it me.

Katherina. Had I a glass, I would.

Petruchio. What, you mean my face.

Katherina. I chafe* you if I tarry. Let me go.

Petruchio. No, not a whit; I find you passing gentle.
'Twas told me you were rough and coy and sullen,
And now I find report a very liar.
For thou art pleasant, gamesome, passing courteous,
But slow in speech, yet sweet as springtime flowers.

*Kate throws a roundhouse but...***

Kate, so straight and slender, and as brown in hue;
As hazelnuts and sweeter than the kernels.
O, let me see thee walk.

*Kate stomps on his foot and he releases her.***

Katherina. Go, fool, and whom thou keepest command.*

chafe: irritate or excite **whom thou keepest command:** keep your orders for your servants
** See section back of script on Stage Combat

Petruchio. In plain terms, Kate, your father hath consented
That you shall be my wife, your dowry 'greed on;
And will you, nill you*, I will marry you.
For I am he am born to tame you, Kate,
And bring you from a wild Kate to a Kate
Comformable as other household Kates.

Enter Baptista, Gremio and Tranio (Lucentio)

Baptista. Now, Signior Petruchio, how speed you with my daughter?

Petruchio. How but well, sir? How but well?

Baptista. Why, how now, daughter Katherina! In your dumps?

Katherina. Call you me daughter? Now, I promise you,
You have showed a tender fatherly regard
To wish me wed to one half lunatic.

Petruchio. Father, 'tis thus: yourself and all the world
That talked of her have talked amiss of her.
For she's not froward but modest as the dove;
And to conclude we have 'greed so well together
That upon Sunday is the wedding day.

Katherina. I'll see thee hanged on Sunday first.

Gremio. Hark, Petruchio: she says she'll see thee hanged first.

will you, nill you: whether you agree or not

Petruchio. 'Tis bargain between us, when we be alone,
That she shall still seemed cursed in company.
I tell you, 'is incredible to believe
How much she loves me. O, the kindest Kate!
She vied upon my neck, and kiss on kiss
That in a twink she won me to her love.
How tame when men and women are alone.
Give me thy hand, Kate: I will unto Venice
to buy apparel 'gainst the wedding day.
Provide the feast, father, and bid the guests.

Baptista. I know not what to say; but give me your hands.
G-d send you joy, Petruchio! 'Tis a match.

Petruchio. Father, and wife, and gentlemen, adieu.
I will to Venice; Sunday comes apace.
We will have rings and things and fine array,
And kiss me, Kate. We will be married o' Sunday.

Petruchio and Katherina exit.

Gremio. And now, Baptista, to your younger daughter:
Now is the day we long have looked for.
I am your neighbor and was suitor first.

Tranio/Luc. And I am one that love her Bianca more
Than words can witness or your thoughts can guess.

Gremio. Youngling, thou canst love so dear as I.

Tranio/Luc. Graybeard, thy love doth freeze.

Gremio. But thine doth fry.

Baptista. Content you* gentlemen; I will compound*
this strife:
'Tis deeds must win the prize, and he, of both,
That can assure my daughter greatest dower
Shall have my Bianca's love.
Say, Signior Gremio, what can you assure her?

Gremio. First, as you know, my house within the city
Is richly furnished with plat and gold:
My hangings all of Tyrian tapestry;
In ivory coffers I have stuffed my crowns;
Fine linen, turkey cushions bossed with pearl,
Valance of Venice gold in needlework,
Pewter and brass, and all things that belong
To house or housekeeping.
Myself am struck in years, I must confess;
And if I die tomorrow, this is hers,
If whilst I live she will be only mine.

Tranio/Luc. That "only" came well in. Sir, list to me:
I am my father's heir and only son;
If I may have your daughter to my wife
I'll leave her houses three or four as good,
Within rich Pisa walls, as any one
Old Signior Gremio has in Padua,
Besides 2000 ducats by the year
Of fruitful land, all which shall be her jointure.

Baptista. I must confess your offer is the best;
And, let your father* make her the assurance,
She is your own; else, you must pardon me,
If you should die before him, where's her dower?

Tranio/Luc. That's but a cavil*: he is old, I young.

content you: be calm **compound:** settle **let your father:** if your father will
cavil: hair-splitting objection

Gremio. And may not young men die as well as old?

Baptista. Well, gentlemen,
I am thus resolved. On Sunday next, you know,
My daughter Katherina is to be married.
Now, on the Sunday following, shall Bianca
Be bride to you if you make the assurance;
If not, to Signior Gremio:
And so I take my leave and thank you both.

Baptista exits.

Gremio. Sirrah young gamester, your father was a fool
To give thee all. Tut! A toy*!

Gremio exits.

Tranio/Luc. Supposed Lucentio must get a father,
called "supposed Vincentio".

Tranio/Luc exits.

a toy: nonsense

ACTOR / DIRECTOR NOTES

ACT III, SCENE 1

Padua. BAPTISTA'S House

*Fun scene, but doesn't add much to plot or character development. So, in order to stage this in the 60-minute range we move directly to -

ACT III, SCENE 2

Padua. Before BAPTISTA'S House

Enter Baptista, Gremio, Katherina, Bianca, Tranio (Lucentio), and Lucentio (Cambio)

Baptista. (To Tranio) Signior Lucentio, this is the 'pointed day
That Katherina and Petruchio should be married,
What will be said? What mockery will be
To want the bridegroom when the priest attends
To speak the ceremonial rites of marriage?

Katherina. Now must the world point at poor Katherina
And say, "Lo! There is mad Petruchio's wife,
If it would please him come and marry me."

Tranio/Luc. Patience, good Katherina and Baptista too.
Upon my life, Petruchio means but well,
Whatever fortune stays him from his word.
Though they be merry, yet withal he's honest.

Katherina. Would Katherina had never seen him, though!

She exits weeping followed by Bianca.

Baptista. Go, girl. I cannot blame thee now to weep,
For such an injury would vex a very saint,
Much more a shrew of thy impatient humor.

Enter Biondello.

Biondello. Master, master! News!

Baptista. Is he come?

Biondello. Why, no sir.

Baptista. What then?

Biondello. He is coming.

Baptista. When will he be here?

Biondello. When he stands where I am and sees you there.

Baptista. Are you mad, man?

Biondello. Petruchio is coming in a new hat and an old jerkin; a pair of old breeches thrice turned; a pair of boots; an old rusty sword ta'en out of the town armory, with a broken hilt and chapeless*.

Enter Petruchio and Grumio.

Petruchio. Where is Kate? Where is my lovely bride?
How does my father? Gentles*, methinks you frown.

Baptista. Why, sir, you know this is your wedding day.
First we were sad, fearing you would not come;
Now sadder that you come so unprovided.
Fie, doff this habit, shame to your estate,
An eyesore to our solemn festival.

chapeless: no metal tip on the sheath **gentles:** gentlemen

Petruchio. Sufficeth I have come to keep my word.
But where is Kate? I stay too long from her;
The morning wears, 'tis time we were to church.

Tranio/Luc. See not your bride in these unreverent robes.
Go to my chamber. Put on clothes of mine.

Petruchio. Not I, believe me. Thus I'll visit her.
To me she's married, not unto my clothes.
But what a fool am I to chat with you
When I should bid good morrow to my bride
And seal the title with a lovely kiss!
He exits.

Tranio/Luc. He hath some meaning in his mad attire.
We will persuade him, be it possible,
To put on better ere he go to church.

Baptista. I'll after him, and see the event of this.

Exit Baptista and Grumio.

Tranio/Luc. I am to get a man,
And he is to be Vincentio of Pisa,
So shall you quietly enjoy your hope,
And marry sweet Bianca with consent.

Enter Gremio.

Tranio/Luc. Signior Gremio. Is the bride and bridegroom coming home?

Gremio. Pray you, Sir Lucentio, when the priest
Should ask if Katherina should be his wife,
"Ay, by gogs wouns*!" quoth he, and swore so loud
That, all amazed, the priest let fall the book,
And, as he stooped again to take it up,
This mad-brained bridegroom took him such a cuff
That down fell priest and book and book and priest.
This done, Signior Petruchio took the bride around the neck
And kissing her lips with such a clamorous smack
That at the parting all the church did echo.
Such a bad marriage never was before.

Enter Petruchio, Katherina, Bianca, Baptista, Hortensio (Licio) and Grumio.

Petruchio. Gentlemen and friends, I thank you for your pains.
I know you think to dine with me today
And have prepared a great store of wedding cheer,
And therefore here I mean to take my leave.

Baptista. Is't possible you will away tonight?

Petruchio. I must away today, before night come.
To my most patient, sweet and virtuous wife,
Dine with my father, drink a health to me,
For I must hence, and farewell to you all.

Tranio/Luc. Let us entreat you stay till after dinner.

Petruchio. It may not be.

Gremio. Let me entreat you.

by gogs wouns: corruption of "by G-d's wounds"

Petruchio. It cannot be.

Katherina. Let me entreat you.

Petruchio. I am content.

Katherina. Are you content to stay?

Petruchio. I am content you shall entreat me to stay,

Katherina. Now, if you love me, stay.

Petruchio. Grumio, my horse!

Katherina. Do what thou canst, I will not go today;
No, nor tomorrow, not till I please myself.
The door is open, sir. There lies your way.

Petruchio. O Kate! Content thee; prithee, be not angry.

Katherina. I will be angry; what hast thou to do*?
(Pause)
Gentlemen, forward to the bridal dinner.
I see a woman may be made a fool
If she had not a spirit to resist.

Petruchio. They shall go forward, Kate, at thy command.
Obey the bride, you that attend on her.
Go to the feast, revel and domineer*,
But for my bonny Kate, she must with me.
I will be master of what is mine own.
She is my goods, my chattels; she is my house,
My horse, my ox, my ass, my anything.

domineer: carouse **what has thou to do:** what do you have to say

Exit Grumio and Petruchio carrying Katherina.

Baptista. Nay, let them go, a couple of quiet ones.

Gremio. Went they not quickly, I should die with laughing.

Tranio/Luc. Of all mad matches never was the like.

Lucentio/Cambio. Mistress, what's your opinion of your sister?

Bianca. That being mad herself, she's madly mated.

Gremio. I warrant him. Petruchio is Kated*.

Baptista. Lucentio, you shall supply the bridegroom's place,
And let Bianca take her sister's room.

Tranio/Luc. Shall sweet Bianca practice how to bride it?

Baptista. She shall, Lucentio. Come gentlemen, let's go.

They all exit

Kated: caught Kate's bad disposition

ACT IV, SCENE 1
PETRUCHIO'S COUNTRY HOUSE

Enter Petruchio and Kate.

Petruchio. Where be these knaves? What no man at door
To hold my stirrup nor to take my horse?
Where is the foolish knave I sent before?

Enter Grumio.

Grumio. Here, sir, as foolish as I was before.

Petruchio. You peasant swain*! You whoreson* malt-horse* drudge!
Did I not bid thee meet me in the park?
Go, rascal, go, fetch my supper in.

Exit Grumio.

(Petruchio sings) Where is the life that late I led?
Where are those - Sit down, Kate, and welcome -
Food, food, food, food!
Why, when, I say? - Nay, good sweet Kate, be merry -
(Sings) *It was the friar of orders grey,*
As her forth walked on his way. Be merry Kate!

Enter Grumio with food.

Petruchio. Come, Kate, sit down. I know you have a stomach.
Will you give thanks, sweet Kate, or else shall I?
What'st this? Mutton?

Grumio. *Ay.*

peasant swain: villainous fellow **whoreson:** good-for-nothing
malt-horse: stupid

Petruchio. 'Tis burnt; and so is all the meat.
How durst you, villain, bring it from the dresser*,
And serve it thus to me that love it not?

Petruchio throws the meat.

Katherina. I pray you, husband, be not so disquiet:
The meat was well, if you were so contented.

Petruchio. I tell thee Kate, 'twas burnt and dried away.
'Tis better 'twere that both of us did fast,
Than feed it with such overroasted flesh.
Be patient; tomorrow't shall be mended,
And for this night we'll fast for company.
Come, I will bring thee to thy bridal chamber.

Petruchio carries her out (See Stage Combat section) as Grumio cleans mess. Curtis soon enters.

Grumio. Where is he?

Curtis. In her chamber, making a sermon of constancy to her:
And rails and swears and rates, that she, poor soul,
Knows not which way to stand, to look, to speak.
Away, away, for he is coming hither.

They exit as Petruchio enters. Petruchio looks about to make sure no one is watching and addresses the audience.

dresser: sideboard

Petruchio. Thus have I politicly begun my reign,
And 'tis my hope to end successfully.
She eat no meat today, nor none shall eat;
Last night she slept not, nor tonight she shall not;
As with the meat, some undeserved fault
I'll find about the making of the bed,
And here I'll fling the pillow, there the bolster,
This way the coverlet, another way the sheets.
Ay, and amid this hurly I intend
That all is done in reverend care of her,
And if she chance to nod, I'll rail and brawl
And with the clamor keep her still awake.
This is a way to kill a wife with kindness,
And thus, I'll curb her mad and headstrong humor.
He that knows better how to tame a shrew,
Not let him speak: *(pause)* 'tis charity to show.

He pauses again waiting for a reply then exits.

ACT IV, SCENE 2

Padua. Before BAPTISTA'S House

Biondello, Tranio (Luc) and Lucentio (Cambio).

Biondello. O master, master! I have watched so long
That I'm dog-weary, but at last I spied
An ancient angel coming down the hill
Will serve the turn.

Tranio/Luc. What is he, Biondello?

Biondello. Master, a marcatante* or a pedant* -
I know not what, but formal in apparel,
In gait and countenance surely like a father.

Lucentio/Cam. And what of him, Tranio?

Tranio/Luc. If he be credulous and trust my tale
I'll make him glad to seem Vincentio,
And give assurance to Baptista Minola
As if he were the right Vincentio.

Exit Lucentio (Cambio) and Bionello.

Enter a Pedant.

Pedant. G-d save you, sir!

Tranio/Luc. And you, sir! You are welcome.
Travel you far on, or are you at the farthest?

Pedant. Sir at the farthest for a week or two,
But then up farther and as far as Rome.

Tranio/Luc. What countryman, I pray?

marcatante: merchant **pedant:** scholar

Pedant. Of Mantua.

Tranio/Luc. Of Mantua, sir! Marry, G-d forbid!
And come to Padua careless of your life?

Pedant. My life, sir! How, I pray? For that goes hard.

Tranio/Luc. 'Tis death for anyone in Mantua
To come to Padua. Know you not the cause?
Your ships are stayed at Venice, and the Duke,
For private quarrel 'twixt your duke and him,
Hath published and proclaimed it openly.

Pedant. Alas, sir! What will you advise me to do?

Tranio/Luc. First, tell me, have you ever been to Pisa?

Pedant. Ay, sir, in Pisa have I often been.

Tranio/Luc. Know you one Vincentio?

Pedant. I know him not but I have heard of him.

Tranio/Luc. He is my father, sir, and sooth to say,
In count'nance somewhat doth resemble you.
To save your life in this extremity,
This favor will I do for you for his sake,
That you are like to Sir Vincentio.
His name and credit shall you undertake.
And in my house you shall be friendly lodged,
Till you have done your business in the city.
If this be court'sy, sir, accept it.

Pedant. O sir, I do; and will repute* you ever
The patron of my life and liberty.

repute: consider

Tranio/Luc. Then go with me to make the matter good.
This, by the way, I let you understand.
My father is here looked for every day
To pass* assurance to a dower in marriage
'Twixt me and one Baptista's daughter here.
In all circumstances* I'll instruct you.
Go with me to clothe you as becomes you.

They exit.

pass: convey **circumstances:** details

ACT IV, SCENE 3
A ROOM IN PETRUCHIO'S HOUSE

Enter Katherina and Grumio.

Grumio. No, no, forsooth; I dare not for my life.

Katherina. The more thy wrong, the more his spite appears.
What, did he marry me to famish me?
Beggars, that come onto my father's door
Upon entreaty a present* alms.
If not, elsewhere they meet with charity.
But I am starved for meat, giddy for lack of sleep,
With oaths kept walking and with brawling fed.
I prithee get me some repast,
I care not what, so it be wholesome food.

Grumio. What say you to a neat's* foot?

Katherina. 'Tis passing good. I prithee let me have it.

Grumio. I fear it is too choleric a meat.
How say you to fat tripe finely broiled?

Katherina. I like it well. Good Grumio, fetch it me.

Grumio. I cannot tell; I fear 'tis choleric.

Katherina. Go, get thee gone, thou false deluding slave.

*She beats Grumio as Petruchio enters with meat.***

Petruchio. Mistress, what cheer?

present: immediately **neat's:** ox's
** See section back of script on Stage Combat

Katherina. Faith, as cold as can be.

Petruchio. Pluck up thy spirits. Look cheerfully upon me.
Your father bids us to Bianca's wedding
And hither must we journey bravely clad.
They tailor stays thy leisure
To deck thy body with his ruffling treasure.

Enter Tailor.

Petruchio. Come tailor, let us see these ornaments;
lay forth the gown.

Enter Haberdasher.
What news withy you, sir?

Haberdasher. Here is the cap your worship did bespeak.

Petruchio. Why, this was molded on a porringer*;
A velvet dish! Fie, fie, 'tis lewd and filthy!

Katherina. O, but I like the cap.

Petruchio. A knack*, a toy, a trick*, a baby's cap.
Away with it! Come, let me have a bigger.

Katherina. I'll have no bigger. This doth fit the time,
And gentlewomen wear such caps as these.

Petruchio. When you are gentler you shall have one too,
And not till then.

Katherina. Why, sir, I trust I may have leave to speak,
And speak I will. I am no child, no babe.
Your betters have endured me say my mind,
And if you cannot, best you stop your ears.

porringer: porridge bowl **knack:** knick-knack **trick:** trifle

Petruchio. I love thee well in that thou likest it not.

Katherina. Love me or love me not, I like the cap.
And it I will have or I will have none.

Exit Haberdasher.

Petruchio. Thy gown? Why, ay. Come, tailor, let us see 't.
O mercy, G-d! what masquing* stuff is here?
What's this? A sleeve? 'Tis like a demi-cannon*.
What! Up and down, carved like an apple tart?
Why, what, in devil's name, tailor, callst thou this?

Tailor. You bid me make it orderly and well,
According to the fashion and the time.

Petruchio. Marry, and did*. But if you be rememb'red,
I did not bid you mar it to the time.
I'll none of it, hence! Make your best of it.

Katherina. I never saw a better-fashioned gown,
More quaint, more pleasing, nor more commendable.
Belike you mean to make a puppet of me?

Petruchio. 'Tis true; he means to make a puppet of thee.

Tailor. She says your Worship means to make a puppet of her.

Petruchio. O monstrous arrogance!
Thou liest, thou thread, thou thimble,
I tell thee, I, that thou hast marred her gown.

masquing: material fit only for a masquerade **demi-cannon:** large cannon
marry, and did: so I did

Tailor. Your worship is deceived. The gown is made
Just as my master had direction.
Grumio gave order how it should be done.

Grumio. I did not bid him to cut it to pieces.

Tailor. Why, here is the note of the fashion to testify.

Petruchio. Read it.

Tailor. "Imprimis*, a loose-bodied gown* -"

Petruchio. Proceed.

Tailor. "With a small compassed* cape."

Grumio. I confess the cape.

Tailor. "With a trunk sleeve*."

Grumio. I confess the sleeves.

Tailor. "The sleeves curiously* cut."

Petruchio. Ay, there's the villainy.
Well, sir, in brief, the gown is not for me.

Grumio. You are i' the right, sir, 'tis for my mistress.

Kate turns away.

Grumio. (Aside) Tailor, I'll pay thee for thy gown
tomorrow;
To no unkindness to his hasty words.

imprimis: in the first place **loose-bodied gown:** worn by prostitutes
compassed : circular **trunk sleeve:** large, wide sleeve
curiously: elaborately

Petruchio. Be gone and say no more. See him out.

Exit Grumio and Tailor.

Petruchio. Well, come my Kate. We will unto your father's
Even in these honest mean habiliments.
Our purses shall be proud, our garments poor,
For 'tis the mind that makes the body rich,
And so the sun breaks through the darkest clouds,
So honor peereth* in the meanest habit*.
What, is the jay more precious than the lark
Because his feathers are more beautiful?
Therefore frolic; we will hence forthwith
To feast and sport us at thy father's house.
Let's see; I think 'tis now some seven o'clock,
And well we may come there by dinnertime.

Katherina. I dare assure you, sir, 'tis almost two
And 'twill be suppertime ere you come there.

Petruchio. It shall be seven ere I go to horse.
Look what I speak or do or think to do,
I will not go today; and ere I do,
It shall be what o'clock I say it is.

Katherina. 'Tis seven, 'tis seven.

Petruchio winks at the audience as they exit.

peereth: shows through **habit:** attire

ACT IV, SCENE 4
Padua. Before BAPTISTA'S House

Enter Tranio (Lucentio) and Pedant (dressed as Vincentio)

Tranio/Luc. Sir, this is the house. Please it you that I call?

Pedant. Ay, what else? And, but I be deceived,
Signior Baptista may remember me,
Near twenty years ago, in Genoa,
Where we were lodgers at the Pegasus.

Tranio/Luc. 'Tis well; and hold your own in any case,
With such austerity as longeth to a father.

Enter Baptista and Lucentio (Cambio)

Tranio/Luc. Signior Baptista, you are happily* met.
(To the Pedant) Sir, this is the gentleman I told you of.
I pray you, stand good father to me now,
Give me Bianca for my patrimony.

Pedant. Soft, son!
Sir, by your leave, having come to Padua
To gather in some debts, my son Lucentio
Made me acquainted with a weighty cause
Of love between your daughter and himself.

happily: per chance

Baptista. Your plainness and your shortness please me well.
Right true it is, your son Lucentio here
Doth love my daughter and she loveth him,
And therefore, if you say no more than this,
That like a father you will deal with him
And pass my daughter a sufficient dower,
The match is made and all is done.

Tranio/Luc. I thank you, sir. Where then do you know best
We be affied*?

Baptista. Not in my house, Lucentio, for you know,
Pitchers have ears, and I have many servants.

Tranio/Luc. Then at my lodging, and it like you,
There doth my father lie, and there this night,
We'll pass the business privately and well.
My boy shall fetch the scrivener* presently.

Baptista. It likes me well. Cambio, hie you home
And bid Bianca make her ready straight.
And, if you will, tell what hath happened:
Lucentio's father is arrived in Padua,
And how she's like to be Lucentio's wife.

Lucentio/Cam. I pray the gods she may with all my heart!

Exit Lucentio (Cambio).

Tranio/Luc. Dally not with the gods, but get thee gone.

Exit all.

affied: formally wed **scrivener:** notary

ACT IV, SCENE 5
A PUBLIC ROAD

Enter Petruchio, Katherina and Hortensio.

Petruchio. Come on, a G-d's name; once more toward our father's.
Good Lord, how bright and goodly shines the moon!

Katherina. The moon? The sun! It is not moonlight now.

Petruchio. I say it is the moon.

Katherina. I know it is the sun that shines so bright.

Petruchio. Now, by my mother's son, and that's myself,
It shall be the moon, or star or what I list
Or e're* I journey to your father's house.

Katherina. I know it is the moon.

Petruchio. Nay, then you lie. It is the blessed sun.

Katherina. Then G-d be blest, it is the blessed sun.

Hortensio. Petruchio, go thy ways; the field is won.

Petruchio. Well, forward, forward! Thus the bowl* shall run.
But soft! Company is coming here.

Enter Vincentio.

Or e're: before **bowl:** ball in a game of bowls

Petruchio. *(To Vincentio)* Good morrow, gentle mistress, where away?
Tell me, sweet Kate, and tell me truly too,
Hast thou beheld a fresher gentlewoman?
Such war of white and red within her cheeks!
Sweet Kate, embrace her for her beauty's sake.

Hortensio. *(Aside)* Will make the man mad, to make a woman of him.

Katherina. Young budding virgin, fair and fresh and sweet,
Wither away, or where is thy abode?
Happy the man, whom favorable stars
Allot thee for his lovely bedfellow!

Petruchio. Why, how now, Kate! I hope thou art not mad;
This is a man - old, wrinkled, faded, withered -
And not a maiden, as thou say'st he is.

Katherina. Pardon, old father, my mistaking eyes,
That have been so bedazzled with the sun
Now I perceive thou art a reverend father;
Pardon, I pray thee, for my mad mistaking.

Petruchio. Do, good old grandsire, and withal make known
Which way thou travelest. If along with us,
We shall be joyful of thy company.

Vincentio. Fair sir, and you, my merry mistress,
That with your strange encounter much amazed me.
My name is called Vincentio, my dwelling, Pisa,
And bound I am to Padua, there to visit
A son of mine, which long I have not seen.

Petruchio. What is his name?

Vincentio. Lucentio, gentle sir.

Petruchio. Happily met, the happier for thy son.
The sister to my wife, this gentlewoman,
Thy son by this hath married. Wonder not
Nor be grieved. She is of good esteem,
Her dowry wealthy, and of worthy birth.

Vincentio. But is this true? Or is it else your pleasure,
Like pleasant travelers, to break a jest
Upon the company you overtake?

Hortensio. I do assure thee, father, so it is.

Petruchio. Come, go along, and see the truth herof;
For our first merriment hath made thee jealous*.
Come.

They all exit.

jealous: suspicious

ACT V, SCENE 1
BEFORE LUCENTIO'S HOUSE

Enter Petruchio, Katherina, Vincentio and Grumio from one side of the stage and enter Pedant from the other.

Vincentio. Is Signior Lucentio within, sir?

Pedant. He's within, sir, but not to be spoken withal.

Vincentio. What if a man bring him a hundred pound or two?

Pedant. Keep your hundred pounds to yourself. He shall need none so long as I shall live.

Petruchio. I pray you tell Signior Lucentio that his father is come from Pisa and is here to speak with him.

Pedant. Thou liest; his father has come from Padua and here looking at you.

Vincentio. Art thou his father?

Pedant. Ay, sir, so his mother says, if I may believe her.

Petruchio (To Vincentio). Why, now now, gentleman! Why, this is flat knavery, to take upon you another man's name.

Pedant. Lay hands on the villain.

Enter Biondello.

Biondello. But who is here? Mine old master, Vincentio! Now we are undone and brought to nothing.

Vincentio. Come hither, crack-hemp*. Have you forgot me?

Biondello. Forgot you! No, sir. I could not forget you, for I never saw you before in all my life.

Vincentio. What, you notorious villain! Didst thou never see thy master's father, Vincentio?

Biondello. What, my old worshipful old master?

Vincentio beats him.

Biondello. Help, help, help! Here's a madman will murder me.

Biondello runs off.

Petruchio. Prithee, Kate, let's stand aside and see the end of this controversy.

They exit.

Enter Pedant, Baptista and Tranio (Lucentio).

Tranio/Luc. Sir, what are you that offer to beat my servant?

Vincentio. What am I, sir? Nay, what are you, sir? O, I am undone! I am undone.

Baptista. What, is the man lunatic?

Tranio/Luc. Sir, you seem a sober ancient gentleman by your habit, but your words show you a madman.

Vincentio. O villain. He is a sailmaker in Bergamo.

crack-hemp: a rogue who deserves hanging

Baptista. You mistake, sir, you mistake. Pray, what do you think is his name?

Vincentio. I have brought him up ever since he was three years old and his name is Tranio.

Pedant. Away, away, mad ass! His name is Lucentio and he is my only son, and heir to the lands of me.

Vincentio. Lucentio! O he hath murdered his master. Lay hold on him. I charge you in the Duke's name! Tell me, thou villain, where is my son, Lucentio?

Enter Lucentio and Bianca as Tranio and Pedant run off.

Lucentio. Pardon, sweet father. (He kneels)

Vincentio. Lives my sweet son?

Bianca. Pardon, dear father.

Baptista. How hast thou offended.
Where is Lucentio?

Lucentio. Here's Lucentio,
Right son to the right Vincentio,
That have by marriage made thy daughter mine
While counterfeit supposes bleared thine eye*.

Vincentio. Where is the damned villain, Tranio,
That faced and braved me in this matter so?

Baptista. Why, tell me, is not this my Cambio?

Bianca. Cambio is changed into Lucentio.

bleared thine eye: hoodwinked you

Lucentio. Love wrought these miracles. Bianca's love
Made me exchange my state with Tranio,
While he did bear my countenance in the town,
And happily I have arrived at the last
Unto the wished haven of my bliss.
What Tranio did, myself enforced him to;
Then pardon him, sweet father, for my sake.

Baptista. Have you married my daughter without asking my good will?

Vincentio. Fear not, Baptista. We will content you. Go to. But I will in to be revenged for this villainy.

Baptista. And I, to sound the depth of this knavery.

Exit Vincentio and Baptista.

Lucentio. Look not pale, Bianca; thy father will not frown.

Exit Lucentio and Bianca as Petruchio and Kate enter.

Katherina. Husband, let's follow to see the end of this ado.

Petruchio. First kiss me, Kate, and we will.

Katherina. What! In the midst of the street?

Petruchio. What! Art thou ashamed of me?

Katherina. No, sir, G-d forbid. But ashamed to kiss.

Petruchio. Why, then let's home again. Come, sirrah, let's away.

Katherina. Nay, I will give thee a kiss; now pray thee, love, stay.

Petruchio. Is not this well? Come, my sweet Kate,
Better once than never, for never too late.

They kiss and exit.

*If time is running short, it is sufficient to conclude with Act V, Scene 1. Some criticize Scene 2 for the way it depicts the role of women. My wife should treat me thus. (That's a joke!) Shakespeare wrote and produced plays without passing judgment but merely held up a mirror to life. Please note the character of Widow is used only in this scene.

ACT V, SCENE 2

Padua. LUCENTIO'S House

Enter Baptista, Vincentio, Gremio, Pedant, Lucentio, Bianca, Biondello, Grumio, Petruchio, Katherina, Hortensio and Widow with Tranio and servants bring in a banquet for all (with all three couples seated together).

Lucentio. Brother Petruchio, sister Katherina,
And thou, Hortensio, with thy loving widow,
Feast with the best and welcome to my house.

Petruchio. Nothing but sit and sit, and eat and eat!

Baptista. Padua affords this kindness, son Petruchio.

Petruchio. Padua affords nothing but what is kind.

Hortensio. For both our sakes I would that word were true.

Petruchio. I faith, Hortensio fears the faith of his widow.

Widow. I am not afeard.

Petruchio. I mean, Hortensio is afeard of you.

Widow. Your husband, being troubled with a shrew
Measure my husband's sorrow by his woe,
And now you know my meaning.

Katherina. A very mean meaning.

Widow. Right, I mean you.

Baptista. How like Gremio these quick-witted folks?

Gremio. Believe me, sir, they butt together well.

Bianca. Head and butt! A hasty-witted body
Would say your head and butt were head and horn.

Vincentio. Ay, mistress bride, hath that awakened you?

Bianca. Ay, but not frightened me; therefore I'll sleep again.

Petruchio. Have at you for a bitter jest or two.

Bianca. Am I your bird? I mean to shift my bush*;
Then pursue me as you draw your bow.
You are all welcome all.

Exit Bianca, Katherina and Widow.

Baptista. Now, in good sadness, son Petruchio,
I think thou hast the veriest shrew of all.

Petruchio. Well, I say no: and therefore, for assurance,
Let's each one send unto his wife,
And he whose wife is most obedient
To come at first when he doth send for her
Shall win the wager which we will propose.

shift my bush: fly to another tree

Hortensio. Content. What's the wager?

Lucentio. Twenty crowns.

Petruchio. Twenty crowns!
I'll venture so much my hawk or hound,
But twenty times so much upon my wife.

Lucentio. A thousand then.

Hortensio. Content.

Petruchio. A match*! 'Tis done.

Hortensio. Who shall begin?

Lucentio. That will I.
Go, Biondello, bid your mistress come to me.

Biondello. I go

Exit Biondello.

Baptista. Son, I'll be your half* Bianca comes.

Lucentio. I'll have no halves; I'll bear it all myself.

Enter Biondello.

Lucentio. How now! What news?

Biondello. Sir, my mistress sends you word,
That she is busy and she cannot come.

a match: agreed **I'll be your half:** share the wager with you

Petruchio. How! She is busy and she cannot come!
Is that an answer?

Gremio. Pray G-d sir, your wife send you not a worse.

Hortensio. Sirrah Biondello, go and entreat my wife
To come to me forthwith.

Petruchio. O ho, entreat her!

Exit Biondello.

Petruchio. Nay, then she must needs come.

Hortensio. I am afraid, sir.
Do what you can, yours will not be entreated.

Enter Biondello with head in bandages.

Hortensio. Now where's my wife?

Biondello. She says you have some goodly jest in hand,
She will not come. She bids you come to her.

Petruchio. Worse and worse. She will not come! O vile,
Intolerable, not to be endured!
Sirrah Grumio, go to your mistress; say
I command her come to me.

Grumio takes a deep breath, crosses himself and exits.

Hortensio. I know her answer.

Petruchio. What?

Hortensio. She will not.

Enter Kate dragging Bianca and the Widow with her.

Petruchio. See where she comes and brings you froward wives
As prisoners to her womanly persuasion.
Katherine, that cap of yours becomes you not.
Off with that bauble, throw it underfoot. (She does so)

Widow. Lord! Let me never have a cause to sigh
Till I be brought to such a silly pass!

Bianca. Fie! What a foolish duty call you this?

Lucentio. I would your duty as foolish too;
The wisdom of your duty, fair Bianca,
Hath cost me a thousand crowns since suppertime.

Bianca. The more fool you for laying* on my duty*.

Petruchio. Katherina, I charge thee, tell these headstrong women
What duty they do owe their lords and their husbands.

Widow. Come, come you're mocking. We will have no telling.

laying: betting **duty:** obedience

Katherina. Fie, fie! Unknit that threat'ning unkind brow,
And dart not scornful glances from those eyes
To wound thy lord, thy king, thy governor.
Thy husband is thy lord, thy life, thy keeper,
Thy head, thy sovereign; one that cares for thee,
And for thy maintenance commits his body
To painful labor both by sea and land,
To watch the night in storms, the day in cold,
Whilst thou liest warm at home, secure and safe;
And craves no other tribute at thy hands
But love, fair looks and true obedience;
I am ashamed that women are so simple
To offer war where they should kneel for peace,
Or seek for rule, supremacy, and sway,
When they are bound to serve, love and obey.
So place your hands below your husband's foot:
In token of which duty, if he please,
My hand is ready; may it do him ease.

Petruchio. Why, there's a wench! Come on and kiss me, Kate.

They kiss. (A stage direction not in any of Shakespeare's works since men played all the female characters.)

Lucentio. Well, go thy ways, old lad, for thou shalt ha 't.

Vincentio. 'Tis a good hearing when children are toward*.

Petruchio. 'Twas I won the wager,
And being a winner, G-d give you good night!

Hortensio. Now go thy ways, thou hast tamed a curst shrew.

toward: obedient

Petruchio. Come, Kate, we'll too bed.

They exit as the lights go down on all.

STAGE COMBAT

'Tis rare for directors to find the time or opportunity to study Stage Combat, so we include some moves gleaned from Joseph Martinez's *COMBAT MIME: A Non-Violent Approach to Stage Violence* (Nelson-Hall Publishing, 1983) for safety and believability. This is the definitive text on stage combat regardless of the level of experience of actors and directors. Even with the simplest of moves there is to be NO IMPROVISATION. Good actors make it look improvised but each move is (and must be) thoroughly rehearsed.

PAGE 13

Petruchio wrings Grumio about the ears:

1. Petruchio reaches to Grumio's LEFT ear with his RIGHT hand with hand wide open.
2. As Pet "grabs" Grumio's ear, he actually puts a closed fist against Grumio's ear.
3. As Pet's hand reaches Grumio's ear and his open hand quickly becomes a fist, Grumio grabs Pet's hand and pushes it against his own ear - to keep Pet from pulling his ear and so they stay together as Grumio thrashes about.
4. Grumio struggles as if Pet is pulling him around. Pet just follows with his hand held steady against Grumio's ear. Grumio is in total control of all movement. Lots of vocalizing.

Petruchio shoves Grumio to the ground:

Pet places his hand on Grumio's shoulder or puts two fingers into Grumio's chest.

Grumio leans in slightly, making eye contact, and pushes off creating the illusion Pet pushed him. Grumio is in total control but important -Pet's hand follows through on the shove so it looks like a push from Pet.

Important for Grumio to not fall on his wrists or tail bone. Side of leg is good.

PAGE 29

Katherina slaps Petruchio: *(So, what's new?)*

First of all let's get the "Just slap me" idea out of the way. It provides no consistency where the slap strikes or proper knap (sound) each time. With adrenaline running, it's easy to end up slapping with fingertips only or leaving an ugly mark on the victim's face the next two scenes.

This is a long-winded explanation, but, like driving a car, you soon get to the point where you put your key in the ignition and take off without giving much thought as to what you're doing.

1. Perspective of Kate upstage of Pet so his back is to the audience. She will slap with her RIGHT hand and he will move his head to his RIGHT side.

2. Just prior to the slap, Pet is holding his left hand up at about the height of his waist - as if he's (like most Italians) talking with his hands.

DETERMINE PROPER DISTANCE - please!
Face each other with feet together. Kate reaches out so her fingertips are about three inches in front of Pet's nose. She then steps back with her LEFT foot and he steps back slightly with his RIGHT foot. Actors are to

take time to set up distance at all rehearsals until they know instinctively the correct positions. This is vital if we are to make sure no one ever gets hurt.

3. Not standing toe-to-toe, Kate's RIGHT foot is displaced between Pet's feet so her RIGHT foot is between his feet. And, be sure to keep proper distance.

4. START SLOW UNTIL YOU GET IT. Both have eye contact so Kate knows Pet is ready. Kate waves her hand past him at a slightly upward angle in a slapping motion but she is far enough away so if Pet does not move she will not hit him. The audience will still be convinced.

5. Victim sells the slap by reaction and knap (slapping sound). As Kate's hand goes past Pet's face he swings his RIGHT hand up and his left hand down making a slapping sound as his hands meet. He immediately tosses his LEFT hand behind him and rests his RIGHT hand on his cheek to comfort the sting. LEFT hand must be behind right away for this to work.

6. Pet is tough so probably won't make a vocal reaction but if there is a choice to make a vocal reaction it MUST be made the moment after the knap or we won't hear the slap.

Initially, you can expect Pet to accidentally slap himself and feel really, really stupid. But it's normal. Or, turn his head the wrong way. Needs to go in the direction his head is slapped.

THE SLAP MOVE REQUIRES A GREAT DEAL OF PRACTICE and must be rehearsed a few times before each performance. Adrenalin from being in front of an audience will mess this simple move up if not thoroughly leaned in the muscles. Audiences will love it and ask after the show how bad it hurt. Milk it, baby. Tell 'em you can take it. You're Petruchio!

PAGE 30

Kate executes a failed roundhouse:

Kate clenches her fist, growls in a most threatening manner, reaches back with her arm and, once eye contact is made and she knows Pet is ready, throws a very menacing round house.

Proper distance has been established so if Pet isn't ready Kate doesn't end up hitting him.

Petruchio ducks as Kate swings past him, missing him. She spins around from the momentum and backs up into him as he steps into her. He holds her as she struggles to get loose.

Foot stomp:

She looks down, lifts her leg and stomps ON THE STAGE just upstage of his foot. Pet vocalizes, lifts his leg, lets her go, etc. Make sure Kate is not directly in front of Pet so heads don't collide if he bends over.

PAGE 44

Petruchio carries Kate off stage:

Fireman's Carry -

Not a bad idea to search the internet for visual aids of what this move looks like.

1. Pet grabs Kate's RIGHT wrist with his LEFT hand and places her RIGHT wrist over his RIGHT shoulder.

2. Pet squats down and keeps his back as straight as possible.

3. Pet places his RIGHT hand between Kate's leg (We're adults!) and behind her RIGHT thigh. *(We're still adults!)*

4. Pet rises (using his leg muscles) and hoists Kate's RIGHT thigh over his RIGHT shoulder. Be sure to keep hold of Kate's arm and leg as rising.

5. OK to gently adjust Kate's weight evenly over his shoulders.

6. While learning, NO STRUGGLE from Kate. Eventually she'll be able to struggle without putting either actor in harm's way. Even if her only struggle comes from vocalizing that will work very nicely.

This particular play works best when done as physically as possible. Your director will use his/her discretion to determine how much or little to use. All that matters is 1) you adhere to proper safety practices at all times and 2) work hard at your craft and never lose sight of the fact you wouldn't be here if you didn't love what you're doing. When you love your craft – your audience will love you. Now go break a leg! Carefully.

PHOTOS & FEEDBACK

You're welcome to send photos to Five Star Publications, Inc. and they'll pass them on to me. I've been able to attend productions with casts as young as second grade up to college level and it's great to see different looks and approaches. If we're interested in using your photos in catalogs, advertising or future scripts we'll seek your permission first.

Even though Five Star Publications retains ownership of suggestions, if any actors, designers or directors have feedback for me to consider before doing reprints, I'd love to hear from you.